Overtake my Heart
Thicc Ric Races for Love

Anita Driver

DEDICATION

This book is dedicated to Daniel Ricciardo who had
nothing to do with the writing of this book.

CONTENTS

DISCLAIMER

This book is a work of fiction. Any resemblance to actual persons, living or dead, or to events that may have occurred, is purely coincidental. The characters and incidents portrayed in this book are the products of the author's imagination or are used fictitiously. No identification with actual persons (living or deceased), places, buildings, and products is intended or should be inferred.

Readers should approach this book as a work of entertainment and understand that the actions, thoughts, and behaviors of the characters are entirely fictitious. The events described within these pages are not based on real-life occurrences or intended to represent any specific individuals or events.

The author and publisher disclaim any responsibility for any loss, injury, or inconvenience caused as a result of reading this book. The reader is advised to exercise caution and critical thinking when interpreting the content and not to attribute the events or behaviors described to real people or situations.

1. THE STARTING LINE

Emily Jensen was no ordinary woman. In a world consumed by fashion, celebrity gossip, and reality TV, she found herself drawn to the roar of engines, the smell of burning rubber, and the thrill of high-speed chases on asphalt circuits. She was an ardent Formula 1 enthusiast, a passion she embraced wholeheartedly, despite the surprised reactions she often received.

Her friends joked that she should have been born with a racing helmet on her head and a checkered flag in her hand. Emily simply laughed along, her hazel eyes shining with an undying love for the sport. Her apartment, a chic, modern space in the heart of the city, bore testament to her obsession, adorned with posters of legendary races, scale models of famous cars, and a collection of biographies of her favorite drivers.

Above all, there was one driver who had won not just races, but Emily's heart as well: Daniel Ricciardo. An Australian racing driver known for his skill behind the wheel and his charismatic personality. She had been smitten with him since his early days in the sport, drawn by his talent, his infectious smile, and his easygoing attitude. Emily knew his stats by heart, had watched every race he'd ever driven, and even had an entire wall in her home dedicated to him, but not in a weird stalker kind of way.

Emily's desire for Daniel Ricciardo was more than just a fangirl's infatuation. Whenever she saw a photo of Daniel, she couldn't help but marvel at his sharp features - the strong jawline, the warm brown eyes, the stubble that added a rugged charm to his face. But what caught her attention the most was his neck, a thicc, muscular testament to the physical demands of being a Formula 1 driver. Each tendon and muscle stood out, giving him an air of raw strength and endurance that was captivating. Emily found herself drawn to the sight, her heart beating faster as she imagined what it would feel like to touch that thick, powerful neck. No other neck could compare. They say a man is 75% water, but not Daniel. He was 75% neck.

His neck was an artful masterpiece of strength and form. It was not the brutish neck of a laborer, but the sculpted refinement of a man who understood the balance of power and grace. Etched with sinew and vein, it was a testament to his discipline, an outward display of the vigor that lay beneath the surface.

The way the muscles flowed, like rolling hills under a landscape of bronzed skin, was entrancing. Each line, each curve, spoke of power in restraint, of a man who knew his strength, yet carried it with a gentle grace that belied the raw might beneath.

The column of Daniel's neck bore the weight of his strong jaw, holding it high with the quiet confidence of a warrior. It was a neck that made her fingers itch to explore, to trace the hard lines and feel the pulsating energy that lay underneath. Each muscle was a story, each line a journey - an atlas of strength and dedication that never failed to ignite her curiosity.

The way his Adam's apple moved when he swallowed or spoke - a subtle, nearly invisible movement - was mesmerizing. The light from the room accentuated his well-defined muscles, giving his neck an almost statuesque appearance.

She longed to feel the warmth of Daniel's skin, the tickle of stubble against her fingertips, and the comforting pulse of his lifeblood beneath. She imagined her lips brushing against his skin, savoring the taste of his sweat and the feel of his muscles tightening at her touch. It was a neck made for kisses that were as much about discovery as they were about passion.

His neck was a symphony of strength and endurance, a testament to his unwavering determination and willpower. It was a part of him that spoke volumes about the man he was – strong, resolute, and infinitely captivating.

His neck had to be a Sky Q or Sky Glass customer with the way it pushed her red button in just the right way.

She needed Daniel in her life. She needed that neck in her life. She craved him the way a dingo farmer craves a cold Foster's beer on a hot, sweaty, Northern Territory day. She needed him the way Nikita Mazepin needed his dad's money to get an F1 seat. But he seemed like a faraway dream.

Besides, she had sworn off dating anyway. After a string of terrible guys, she had put her body and her heart in parc fermé. No one was allowed to touch, except for maybe Inspector Seb[i].

Little did she know, her passion was about to lead her to a thrilling encounter that would change her life.

It was a typical Tuesday evening for Emily, sprawled on her plush, grey couch, watching a replay of the 2018 Chinese Grand prix, a race she had watched Danny win so many times. "Get it girl, get it" she mouthed along with Daniel's voice on the team radio.[ii]

Suddenly, Emily's cellphone buzzed on the coffee table, shattering the focus she had on the television screen. Glancing at the caller ID, she saw it was her friend Lisa, a petite, vivacious woman who worked as the guest services manager at one of the city's most luxurious hotels.

"Lisa? What's up?" Emily asked, hitting the mute button on the TV remote.

"You won't believe who just checked into the hotel, Em," Lisa squealed in excitement. Emily could hear the chatter of hotel staff in the background.

"Who?" Emily asked, her curiosity piqued. Lisa was not one to get easily excited. Over the years, she had seen countless celebrities stroll through the hotel's grand lobby.

"Your dream man, Emily. Daniel Ricciardo," Lisa finally spilled the beans, barely able to contain her excitement.

Emily's heart skipped a beat. "Are you serious?" she asked, her mind racing faster than the cars on her muted TV screen.

"As a heart attack! He's here for the Wrangler

Jeans Coca Cola Kentucky Grand Prix. And guess what? He'll be here all week." [iii]

Emily's mind was spinning. Daniel Ricciardo was in her city, at Lisa's hotel, just a few miles away from where she sat. It felt surreal, like a dream she had replayed countless times in her head.

"Oh my god... that's amazing, Lisa. Thank you for telling me," Emily managed to utter, her mind already hatching a plan.

As she hung up the phone, Emily couldn't help but smile. Would this be her chance to finally meet the Australian man of her dreams? It just vege-might be! And she was not going to let this opportunity slip away.

After the phone call, Emily sat motionless on her couch, her mind spinning with a million thoughts. Daniel Ricciardo, and his neck, were just a few miles away. The knowledge was both exhilarating and terrifying. She had spent countless hours dreaming of a chance to meet him, and now the opportunity had presented itself in the most unexpected way.

She knew she had to make something happen. A plan began to form in her mind. She could visit Lisa at the hotel under some pretext, and just happen to run into Daniel. Yes, that could work. It was a long shot, but it was worth a try. After all, fortune favors the bold, she told herself.

The next day, Emily woke up with a sense of purpose she hadn't felt in a long time. She took extra care in picking out her outfit: a simple yet elegant black dress that was professional enough for a meeting but casual enough for a hotel lobby. She let her auburn hair fall in soft waves, applied a touch of makeup, and slipped on her favorite pair of black heels. Looking at herself in the mirror, she felt a surge of confidence. She looked good and felt even better.

She texted Lisa, telling her she was dropping by the hotel to catch up over lunch, but Lisa saw right through the plan. "Are you coming here to see Daniel? Are you planning a meet cute? Are you going to try to play his didgeridoo?!" Lisa demanded to know.

After a little razzing, Lisa relented and agreed to help Emily with her plan. As Emily left her apartment, she felt a nervous flutter in her stomach. She had no way of knowing whether her plan would work, but she was determined to try.

The drive to the hotel was a blur. Her hands gripped the steering wheel tightly, her heart pounded in her chest, and her mind played out different scenarios. Would she actually bump into Daniel? What would she say? Would he be polite? Dismissive? Would he recognize the admiration in her eyes? Would he adore her neck as much as she adored his? Each question made her more nervous, but the prospect of meeting Daniel Ricciardo was too tantalizing to resist.

As she parked her car in the hotel's parking lot, she took a deep breath. This was it. She was about to walk into a hotel where Daniel Ricciardo was staying. She was about to possibly meet the man who had unknowingly been such a huge part of her life. Emily felt a strange mix of excitement and nervousness, but above all, she felt ready. This was her moment, and she was not going to let it slip away.

---

iIt was different back then. Less woke. It was a time when a world champion could have his way with any car in the pit lane. You could just start kissing them. It's like a magnet. Just kiss. You wouldn't even wait. If you were a star, they'd let you do it. You could do anything. Grab 'em by the rear wing. But not anymore. Just ask Max.

[ii] Second best radio message of that race, after "see you fucking later son".

[iii] Rawe Ceek lasts a whole week.

2. A CHANCE ENCOUNTER

The grand lobby of the hotel was bustling with activity. Emily took a moment to soak it all in – the elegant décor, the lively chatter, the occasional tinkling laughter echoing off the marble floors. Somewhere in this opulence, Daniel Ricciardo was staying. The thought sent a shiver of anticipation down her spine.

She spotted Lisa across the room, waving at her from behind the front desk. Emily waved back, signaling that she would be there in a moment. She took a deep breath, steadying herself. Her plan was simple: wander around the lobby as if she were waiting for Lisa, and hopefully, bump into Daniel.

With a last glance in the mirror to check her appearance, Emily started her leisurely stroll around the lobby. She tried to look casual, her eyes discreetly scanning the area for any sign of Daniel. After a few minutes, she spotted him. There he was, Daniel Ricciardo, just as handsome in person, engrossed in a conversation with what appeared to be a team member.

Emily's heart pounded in her chest, and for a moment, she considered abandoning her plan. But then she remembered all those years of admiring him from afar, all the races she had watched, the wins and losses she had celebrated and mourned with him. And then there was that muscular neck. This was her chance, and she was not going to back down now.

She timed her steps, aiming to casually cross paths with Daniel. As she neared him, she pretended to stumble slightly, bumping into him lightly.

"Oh! I'm so sorry," she exclaimed, her cheeks flushing with a mix of embarrassment and excitement.

Daniel turned around, his surprise quickly melting into a warm smile. "No worries at all. Are you alright?" he asked, his Australian accent as charming in person as it was on TV.

Emily found herself looking into Daniel Ricciardo's eyes, and for a moment, the world around her seemed to fade away. She was finally face-to-face with the man she had admired for years, and it was more thrilling than any race she had ever watched. This was it, her moment with Daniel Ricciardo. It was time to make it count.

"I'm alright," Emily responded, regaining her footing. "I think I out braked myself there! But honestly, it's these shoes." She looked down at her heels and then flashed a playful grin back up at Daniel. "These heels can be as unpredictable as a new set of tires on a cold track."[iv]

His laughter echoed through the lobby, a warm, inviting sound that set Emily's heart racing. "I see what you did there," he said, his eyes twinkling with amusement. "You're a fan of the sport?"

Emily nodded, her nerves gradually replaced by a growing confidence. "Indeed, I am. Have been following your career since you were just a rookie, back with HRT."

Daniel's eyebrows shot up in surprise, and Emily could see a spark of interest light up in his eyes. "You've been with me through the pit stops and podiums, then," he remarked, clearly impressed.

Their conversation took off like a race car on the final lap. They navigated through topics of past races, legendary tracks, and the thrilling unpredictability of the sport. Emily cleverly laced her language with racing jargon, her remarks punctuated with playful innuendos that kept Daniel both engaged and entertained.

"You know, in a lot of ways, racing is just like a good conversation," she said at one point, her eyes twinkling with mischief. "It's all about the chemistry, the timing, and knowing when to make your move."

Daniel laughed at that, the sound warm and genuine. "Well, then," he replied, a playful grin on his face. "I must say, this conversation is definitely a pole position one."

As the minutes ticked away, Emily found herself more and more drawn to the man before her. She had admired Daniel Ricciardo the racer for years, but now she found herself equally intrigued by Daniel Ricciardo the man. He was charming, witty, and shared her passion for a sport that defined her life. And that neck. Damn.[v]

And Daniel seemed to share the feeling. It wasn't every day he met a fan who could match his racing anecdotes with ones of their own, who understood the excitement of a perfect lap, the frustration of a pit stop gone wrong[vi], and the heart-pounding thrill of a photo finish.

As their conversation came to a close, Emily knew she had made an impression. She had taken a chance, made her move, and it had paid off. The race, it seemed, was just getting started.

Then Emily felt an unexpected pang of disappointment. She'd been captivated by their shared passion, their easy banter, and most of all, the genuine and charming man Daniel turned out to be. However, she knew this moment couldn't last forever.

Just as she was about to suggest they should probably part ways, Daniel beat her to it, his eyes sparkling with a mix of anticipation and excitement. "Emily, our conversation has been the highlight of my day. It's not every day I meet someone who loves racing as much as I do and can keep up with my pit lane stories."

Emily felt her cheeks warm under his praise. "Thank you, Daniel. I've had a fantastic time too."

He paused for a moment, seeming to gauge her response before continuing. "I was wondering if you'd like to continue our conversation over dinner? There's an Outback Steakhouse nearby. I would love share the food of my people with you."

Emily was momentarily stunned. Was this really happening? Was Daniel Ricciardo, the man she'd admired from afar for so long, inviting her to dinner?

"I'd love that, Daniel," she replied, her voice steady despite the thrill of excitement coursing through her. "I've always wanted to try a bloomin' onion."

Daniel laughed, clearly pleased by her response. "Perfect! It's a date then. Let's say, eight o'clock?"

Emily nodded, her heart fluttering with the promise of the evening to come. "Eight sounds great."

As she walked away, Emily couldn't help but replay the encounter in her mind. She was going to dinner with Daniel Ricciardo. This was more than she could have ever hoped for, and she couldn't wait to see where this race would lead.

---

iv Can't wait until they get rid of tire blankets. It's going to be crashtastic.

v A neck haiku:
Strength in Daniel's nape,
Sculpted, firm like hero's cape,
Sexy form takes shape.

vi Monaco. Nuff said.

3. THE FIRST DATE

At eight o'clock sharp, Daniel arrived to pick up Emily for their date. Seeing him standing there, looking casually handsome in a pair of dark jeans and a button-down shirt, Emily's heart fluttered with anticipation. His neck glistened in the evening air. His warm smile set her at ease, and they set off for the Outback Steakhouse.

The restaurant was lively with chatter and the comforting aroma of grilled steak. They were seated at a quiet corner booth, where they had the perfect balance of privacy and a view of the bustling eatery.

The night kicked off with laughter as Daniel insisted Emily try the Bloomin' Onion, a classic Australian starter. "It's not an authentic Aussie experience without it," he said, his eyes gleaming with mischief.[vii] Emily played along, and they both laughed as she took an exaggeratedly cautious bite, only to proclaim it delicious.

The laughter set the tone for the rest of the evening. They shared stories about their favorite races, debated over the best drivers of all time, and swapped anecdotes from their lives. Emily found herself opening up to Daniel in a way she rarely did with others. There was something about him that made her feel comfortable, seen, and appreciated.

Their conversation flowed as smoothly as an Adrian Newey designed car in the wind tunnel, moving from racing to more personal topics. Emily learned about Daniel's childhood in Australia, the various pet kangaroos he had owned, his journey into racing, and his dreams for the future. In return, she shared her own story, her passion for the sport, and her aspirations.

Throughout the night, their chemistry was undeniable. They found themselves lost in deep conversation, their mutual passion for racing serving as the initial spark that had ignited into something more personal, more intimate.

As the evening wore on, Emily realized how much she was enjoying Daniel's company. His charm, his wit, his genuine interest in her stories - all these things made her feel a connection she hadn't anticipated. It was as if they had known each other for years rather than just a few hours.

The night ended with Daniel walking Emily to her car, the air between them electric with shared laughter and unspoken connection. As she drove home, Emily found herself replaying the night in her head, the smile on her face a testament to the wonderful time she had spent with Daniel Ricciardo. It had been an unforgettable date, and she could only hope it was the first of many more to come.

Back in the comfort of her own home, Emily replayed the events of the night, her mind a whirlwind of thoughts. She had had an amazing time with Daniel, there was no denying that. His charm, his humor, his authenticity - all of it had drawn her in.

Yet, amidst the fluttering excitement, a nagging doubt began to creep in. She couldn't help but remember the stories she'd heard about Daniel Ricciardo, the playboy. His charm had won over countless women before her, and his reputation for fleeting romances was as well-known as his racing prowess. Just how many women had put their hands on his boomerang?

Could someone like him, who was used to the glamorous and transient lifestyle of a Formula 1 driver, truly be interested in someone like her? She was just an ordinary woman who happened to love the same sport he did. Was their connection real, or was she just another pit stop in his fast-paced life?

She paced her living room, wrestling with her feelings. On one hand, she was thrilled about the fantastic time they had shared, the undeniable connection they had established. She had been attracted to Daniel for a long time, but their shared passion for racing and their deep conversations had ignited a flame that was different from her previous admiration.

On the other hand, she was afraid of getting hurt. She didn't want to be another name on his list, another woman charmed and then forgotten. She valued herself too much to let that happen.

Emily sat down on her couch, her mind racing. She was falling for Daniel Ricciardo, there was no doubt about that. But could she trust him? Could she trust his intentions, his words, his actions?

The questions spun in her head like Nikita

Mazepin on a wet track. Or a dry track. She knew she had to tread carefully, for her heart was at stake. And yet, the thrill of what could be was too enticing to resist. She was at a crossroads, and she had to decide which way to steer.

The following days were filled with an internal tug-of-war. Emily found herself daydreaming about Daniel, about their conversation, his laugh, the way he looked at her. Her heart yearned for more, yet her mind kept reeling her back, reminding her of the possible heartache that could come with falling for a man like Daniel.

The next evening, while caught up in her thoughts, her phone buzzed. It was a text from Daniel. He had just finished a neck workout with his trainer, and was inviting her over to his hotel for a nightcap. Her heart fluttered at the invitation, and she found herself typing a response before her mind could interfere.

She dressed up in a casual but chic outfit and headed to the hotel. Seeing Daniel again, his warm smile welcoming her, all her doubts seemed to melt away. They spent the evening talking, laughing, and sipping on their drinks, the chemistry between them as palpable as ever.

As the evening grew late, Emily decided it was time to head home. She said her goodbyes to Daniel, ignoring the disappointment flashing in his eyes. As she walked towards her car, her heart felt heavy. She was leaving behind a man she was deeply attracted to, a man she connected with on so many levels, all because of fear.

Halfway to her car, she stopped. She looked back at the hotel, its lights glowing in the night. An internal battle raged within her. She was afraid of getting hurt, yes. But she was also afraid of letting go of something that could be truly special.

With a deep breath, she turned around. She walked back into the hotel and took the elevator up to Daniel's floor. Standing in front of his door, she felt a mix of fear and anticipation. Without knocking, she opened the door to Daniel's room.

"Not now, Max. I'm not in the mood tonight" said Daniel, before looking up from his phone. "Oh… Emily, is everything alright?" he said, realizing his mistake.[viii]

"Yes," she said, her voice steady. "I just realized I wasn't ready for the night to end."

Daniel offered Emily a glass of Ric3 Shiraz from St Hugo[ix], but she politely declined, her gaze locked with his. There was an unspoken understanding between them, a shared desire that neither of them could ignore any longer.

Slowly, Daniel closed the distance between them. His hand gently brushed against her cheek, causing her to close her eyes at the tender touch. "Emily," he whispered, his voice filled with a mix of desire and admiration.

When she opened her eyes, she saw the same emotions reflected back in his. She reached up, touching his face, tracing the lines of his stubble, his jaw, his lips, his neck.[x] The anticipation was like the revving of engines, the countdown before the lights go out, and the race begins.

Their lips met in a slow, explorative kiss. It was as if they were taking their time, savoring the moment, just as one would savor the adrenaline rush of a race. Daniel's hands found their way to Emily's waist, pulling her closer, deepening the kiss.

They moved instinctively, a dance as synchronized as a pit stop[xi], each action leading seamlessly to the next. Their clothes were shed, left in a trail leading to the bedroom. Their bodies entwined,˙ lost in the exploration of each other, every touch igniting sparks of pleasure.

The world outside ceased to exist. All that mattered was the here and now, the shared intimacy, the connection that transcended their physical closeness. Emily found herself lost in Daniel, his touch, his scent, his taste. And she felt him respond with equal passion, his actions speaking volumes about his desire for her.

She loved the way his body felt on top of hers. It felt like the downforce of a thousand rear wings, all at once.[xii]

The night was filled with whispered words, tender touches, and passionate exchanges. It was a night where they crossed the line from friends to lovers, a night where Emily let go of her fears and surrendered to her feelings for Daniel.

As the first light of dawn seeped into the room, Emily lay in Daniel's arms, their bodies tangled in the sheets. His warm body draped over her like a tire blanket. She looked up at him, his face relaxed in sleep, his chest rising and falling rhythmically. She had never seen him so peaceful, so vulnerable. It was a side of him she had never expected to see, and it made her fall for him even more.

As she closed her eyes, nestled against him, Emily knew she had made the right decision. She had taken a leap of faith, and it had led her to a night she would always remember. She fell asleep with a content sigh, her heart beating in sync with Daniel's, hopeful for what   the   future   might   bring.

---

vii The Bloomin' Onion is a traditional aboriginal dish that has been recognized with UNESCO World Heritage Status.
viii What happens in the paddock, stays in the paddock.
ix Quite possibly the world's finest wine made by a race car driver.
x A neck sonnet:
Upon Daniel's form, a structure grand,
A neck of might, sculpted by skilled hand.
Muscles that flex in the soft candle light,
A testament to his strength, power and might.

No marble statue could match such a sight,
In his presence, the stars seem less bright.
Like a column of marble, robust and refined,
It speaks of a character steady, inclined.

His tenderness, masked in sinew so bold,
A story of manliness, waiting to be told.
Yet beneath the steel, a softness resides,
In Daniel's strong neck, gentle heart abides.

A vision of strength, a paragon of grace,
His muscular neck, the most handsome place.
xi Not a Ferrari pit stop, obviously.
xii The down force of 1,000 rear wings would be roughly 700,000 kg

4. THE AFTERMATH

The next day, Emily found herself sitting across from Lisa at their favorite café. Lisa's face was a picture of anticipation, her eyes sparkling with curiosity. She had been Emily's confidante, her sounding board for as long as she could remember. She had been there through every crush, every heartbreak, every moment of joy and despair. And now, she was waiting to hear about Emily's unexpected encounter with Daniel Ricciardo.

Emily took a sip of her coffee, her mind racing with memories of the previous night. The laughter, the deep conversations, the undeniable chemistry - it was all too surreal.

"So, spill it, Em," Lisa prodded, leaning across the table. "How was it? I mean, Daniel Ricciardo! That's like a dream come true, isn't it?"

Emily let out a soft laugh, her mind replaying the

moments she had shared with Daniel. "It was... amazing," she admitted. "He was charming, funny, and incredibly easy to talk to. We had dinner at an Outback Steakhouse, and he was so passionate about sharing his love for Australian cuisine. It felt like we were the only two people in the world."

Lisa's eyes widened, her excitement palpable. "And...?" she pressed, a mischievous grin on her face.

Emily blushed, her heart fluttering at the memory of their intimate encounter. "And... nothing happened. At least not that night. But last night, he invited me to his hotel for a drink," she confessed, her voice barely above a whisper. "One thing led to another, and... well, you know."

Lisa let out a squeal of delight, her grin widening. "Oh my god, Emily! Tell me everything! How big was his front wing, if you know what I mean? Was he only good for one lap or can he handle an entire race distance? Did he spray his bottle of champagne? Did you make him sweat like a high performance athlete? Sweat baby, geee geee geee, raaaaah, sweat baby, woo!"

"Inappropriate, Lisa!" Emily scolded. "I don't kiss and tell."

"Ok, fine. This is incredible! But... how do you feel about it all? I mean, he's Daniel Ricciardo, the playboy racer. The honey badger has honey pots in every city. Are you okay with that?"

Emily's smile faltered slightly, her heart heavy with a mixture of excitement and apprehension. "I don't know, Lisa," she admitted. "I mean, it was amazing. He was amazing. But his reputation... I can't help but wonder if I'm just another notch on his belt."

Lisa reached across the table, squeezing Emily's

hand reassuringly. "Well, whatever happens next, remember you're a catch, Emily. And if he doesn't see that, then he's not worth your time."

Emily nodded, a small smile tugging at her lips. Lisa was right. She had to trust her instincts, trust herself. She had taken a leap of faith, and now, all she could do was wait and see where this unexpected pit stop would lead her.

5. RACE DAY

The roar of the crowd, the smell of burning rubber, the adrenaline-fueled tension - it was all part of the thrilling tableau that is a Formula 1 race. But today, as Daniel prepared for the race, there was an added dimension to his usual pre-race routine. He couldn't stop thinking about Emily.

Images of the previous night flashed in his mind - her laughter, the deep conversations they had, the feel of her skin against his. The memory of their shared passion fueled his determination, igniting a fire within him like never before.

As he got into his car, he felt a strange sense of calm. The usually daunting circuit seemed less intimidating, the competition less fierce. He felt invincible, empowered. Emily had unlocked something in him, something that was making him view the race in a different light. Maybe today was the day he would finally best his teammate, two-time world champion Nicholas Latifi.[xiii]

The lights went off, and the race began. Daniel was in his element, his car moving like an extension of himself. Every turn, every acceleration, every brake - it was all executed with a precision and confidence that was remarkable even for him.

He could hear the cheers of the crowd, the voices of his team over the radio, but it all seemed like a distant hum. All he could think of was Emily, her words of encouragement, her belief in him.

As he crossed the finish line, Tim Apple waived the checkered flag with a limp wrist and the crowd erupted into cheers. Daniel had won the race, a victory that was as much a testament to his skill as a driver as it was to the transformative power of the previous night with Emily. He lifted his trophy high, his heart pounding with elation, but he knew that this victory was more than just a win on the track. It was a confirmation of his feelings for Emily, feelings that had made him not just a better man but a better driver as well.

Despite the victory on the track, life off the track moved with relentless speed for Daniel Ricciardo. Within hours of his triumph, he had to pack up and fly to the next city for the upcoming race. The life of a Formula 1 driver was an unending cycle of races, flights, and hotel rooms. Sure, things were easier now that Liberty Media had moved every race to the US, but he still was constantly traveling from city to city and coast to coast.

Daniel had to leave abruptly, the schedules and obligations of his career leaving him no time for a proper goodbye. A text message was all he could manage, a few words to let Emily know he had to leave, a promise to call her soon.

Back in her apartment, Emily read the text message over and over again, her heart heavy with a mix of emotions. She was proud of Daniel, thrilled at his victory, but she couldn't shake off the feeling of disappointment. Their night of passion, their deep conversations, their shared laughter - it all felt like a distant dream now.

She understood the demands of his career. She had always known that the life of a Formula 1 driver was a nomadic one. But the sudden departure, the curt goodbye, it all left her with a feeling of emptiness.

She found herself staring at her phone, waiting for a call that didn't come, replaying their moments together in her mind. She wanted to believe in Daniel, in his promise to call her, but the reality of his absence was hard to ignore.

As the days turned into a week, and then another, Emily was left grappling with her feelings. She was falling for Daniel, there was no denying that. But his absence, his silence, it all made her question her place in his life.

Was she just another woman in a long line of transient relationships for Daniel? Or was there something more, something real between them? The uncertainty hung over her like a Russian rain cloud that only Nikita Mazepin could recognize[xiv], casting a shadow over her memories of their time together. She was left waiting, hoping, and wondering if Daniel would ever return to her life.

After two weeks of silence, Emily finally decided to take matters into her own hands. She couldn't keep waiting for a call that may never come, couldn't keep holding onto a hope that was fading with each passing day. To put her life on pause, waiting for Daniel to call made her feel as useless as a set of wet tires at the Bahrain Grand Prix.

She spent a whole afternoon flipping through her collection of Formula 1 memorabilia, thinking about the other drivers. Was there another driver who could be her new obsession? She went through the grid, one by one.

What about Lewis? She had always fancied him, but the violent porpoising effect of his car in 2022 had left him a battered, broken man. What about Charles? He probably was too focused on his music career to make time for her. Lance? Too sticky from maple syrup. Fernando? He'd never leave Taylor Swift for me, Emily thought. George? He was talented for sure. But a man who refuses to wear a shirt is a man you can't take anywhere. Pierre? He was just so… French.

Each driver had their own appeal and their own unique charm, but also their own flaws. She contemplated shifting her focus, trying to find in them what she had found in Daniel. She even considered attending the upcoming McDonald's Cowboy Freedom Eagle Oklahoma Grand Prix[xv], hoping that a new environment, a new driver to root for, could help her move on.

But as she sat there, surrounded by racing posters and memorabilia, she couldn't shake off the image of Daniel. His smile, his warmth, the connection they had - it all kept coming back to her. Despite the silence, despite the distance, she realized that her feelings for Daniel were far deeper than a mere infatuation. And even though she was contemplating moving on, her heart wasn't quite ready to let go of Daniel Ricciardo.

In the end, she decided to give herself more time. She would try to move on, try to find a new infatuation. But she knew that it would take more than just a decision to truly let go of Daniel. Because despite everything, a part of her still clung onto the hope that one day, her phone would ring, and on the other end, she would hear Daniel's voice once again.

Days turned into weeks and still, Emily's phone remained silent. Each vibration, each notification, sent a jolt of hope coursing through her, only to be replaced by disappointment when it wasn't Daniel. She couldn't help but check her phone constantly, praying for a message, a call, any sign that he hadn't forgotten her.

She kept herself busy to distract from the pain. She tried browsing the humorous posts on the Formula Dank subreddit, but the memes about Chadlonso[xvi] and a certain Monaco-based YouTuber who beat Lewis in equal machinery did nothing to cheer her up. She threw herself into her work, went out with friends, even tried dating other people. But every time she found herself alone, her mind would drift back to Daniel - his smile, his laugh, the way his eyes lit up when he talked about racing.

Her friends tried to console her. "That Aussie boy is a didgeri-don't" Lisa told her. "The man literally drinks from a shoe. GROSS!" [xvii]

Other friends told her that it was Daniel's loss, that she deserved someone who would appreciate her.

But their words, though well-intentioned, only seemed to amplify her heartbreak.

She started to question everything. Had their connection been real? Had she misread his intentions? Or had she been just another fling in his glamorous, jet-setting life? The uncertainty was worse than the silence. It gnawed at her, made her question her self-worth.

And as the reality of Daniel's absence sunk in, she couldn't help but feel a sense of loss. Not just for the man she had fallen for, but for the connection they had shared, for the promise of what could have been, and also for his neck. She had opened her heart to Daniel, let him see a side of her that she rarely showed anyone. And now, it felt like that vulnerability had been in vain.

As she laid in bed each night, staring at the ceiling, she could almost hear the distant roar of the F1 cars, could almost see Daniel behind the wheel, his focus solely on the race. And it broke her heart to think that while he was out there, living his dream, she was left behind, nursing a heart more broken than Nikita Mazepin's car after crashing out of his first race on turn three of lap one.

But despite the heartbreak, she knew she had to keep moving forward. She had to find a way to heal, to reclaim the part of her that she felt like she had lost to Daniel. She was not just a Formula 1 enthusiast who had fallen for a driver. She was Emily - strong, independent, and capable of overcoming heartbreak. And she was determined to prove that to herself, even if it meant facing the pain of Daniel's silence each   day.

[xiii] I am from the future. This actually happens. Trust me.

[xiv] In the 2021 Russian Grand Prix, Nikita Mazepin recognized the Russian rain clouds before anyone else and was the first car to switch to inters, giving him an advantage over the rest of the grid propelling him to a last place finish.

[xv] This is a far less ridiculous name than the 2023 Formula 1 Qatar Airways Gran Premio Del Made In Italy e Dell'Emilia-Romagna with Cheese.

[xvi] This is an unstoppable hype train

[xvii] Do not try this at home. Athlete's Tongue is a very serious fungal infection that afflicts dozens of Aussies every year.

6. THE STRUGGLE

Daniel Ricciardo, known for his unflappable demeanor and unmatched concentration, was finding it increasingly difficult to focus on racing. Every city he flew into, every track he raced on, seemed to remind him of Emily. Her laughter echoed in his mind, her words of encouragement became his mantra, her image, a haunting presence that was inescapable. She had certainly laid down a lot of rubber on his heart.

He tried to shake her off, to lose her in the whirlwind of his racing life. There were other women, other cities, other races. It's like Daniel's uncle used to say about women: "there's always another shrimp on the barbie, and there's always another girl." But still he was having trouble forgetting her. He was living the dream of every aspiring racer - a life of speed, fame, and endless adventure. But somehow, it all felt hollow, incomplete.

Every conversation seemed dull in comparison to their late-night talks. Every race felt less exciting without her there to share it with. Every woman he met seemed to lack the spark that Emily had ignited in him.

The relentless pace of his career, which once brought him exhilaration, now seemed to underscore his loneliness. The silence of his hotel rooms was deafening, the absence of her warmth, unbearable.

He tried to fill the void with more racing, more parties, more women and more Tim Tams. He told himself that he could forget her, that he could move on. But the more he tried to push her away, the more his mind drifted back to her.

His performance on the track began to suffer. His usually sharp instincts were blunted, his impeccable precision, unsteady. The once invincible Daniel Ricciardo was faltering, his thoughts constantly straying to a certain someone back home. It was as if he was stuck behind her in a DRS train, unable to get out of her dirty air.

His team noticed the change, attributing it to fatigue, to the pressures of the sport. But Daniel knew better. He was not tired, not burnt out. He was haunted - haunted by thoughts of Emily, by the memory of their shared passion, by the regret of leaving her behind.

As he stood on the podium of yet another race, his mind was not on the cheering crowd or the trophy in his hand. It was on Emily. And for the first time in his career, Daniel Ricciardo found himself questioning his choices, wondering if the thrill of the race was worth the ache in his heart.

Daniel's thoughts of Emily were not just affecting his personal life, but were starting to seep onto the racetrack as well. The man who once held the reputation of being unwaveringly focused, a driver who could push all personal issues aside when he put on his helmet, was now showing signs of vulnerability. This was not the honey badger the world was used to seeing.

His start times were slower, his reactions were delayed, and even his maneuvers, which once drew applause from even his fiercest critics, were now being questioned. His team was growing concerned, unable to pinpoint the cause of this sudden drop in performance.

Race after race, Daniel tried to regain his form, but it was as if he was driving through a fog. His mind kept drifting back to Emily - her smile, her words, the feel of her touch. The roar of the engines, the screech of tires, the cheering of the crowd, all seemed to fade into the background as memories of Emily consumed him.

His fans were puzzled, the media was speculating, and his rivals were gaining ground. The once-dominant force on the track was now struggling to finish in the top five. The descent was gradual but undeniable. Daniel Ricciardo, the man known for his infectious grin and racing prowess, was losing his spark.

"Ric, you need to get your head in the game" his exasperated race engineer told him. "If you don't, you'll end up like Nikita Mazepin, shoveling manure in your dad's fertilizer factory in Siberia!"

He watched race footage, analyzed his performance, had countless meetings with his team. But no matter how hard he tried, he couldn't shake off his feelings for Emily. She was there, in every corner he turned, in every finish line he crossed, in every trophy he held.

His heart was on a different race, one that had nothing to do with speed or circuits, but everything to do with a woman who had touched his soul. The realization was as surprising as it was unsettling. He was not just missing Emily, he was yearning for her. And this yearning was costing him his racing form.

To help him sort through his feelings, Daniel enlisted the help of professional Twitch streamer and former teammate Lando Norris.

"Look Daniel, I'm only 17 years old," Lando reminded him. "And I've spent almost all of my 17 years playing video games, so I don't really have any experience with women. But if you have such strong feelings for Emily, maybe you should consider pursuing her."

The playboy racer, the man who lived life in the fast lane, the man with the golden neck was now being forced to confront a new reality - his feelings for Emily were far deeper than he had ever imagined. And until he could reconcile with those feelings, his life on the track would continue to spiral into a Mazepin-esque disaster. The chase for Emily had begun, and it was a race unlike any Daniel had ever run.

6. THE PURSUIT

The decision was made - Daniel had to win Emily back. It was not just a matter of the heart, but of his racing career as well. But the path ahead was not going to be easy. His abrupt departure, his weeks of silence, and his playboy reputation were all stacked against him. Winning a race was one thing; winning back the trust and affection of a woman he had hurt was entirely another.

He pondered over how he could possibly make amends. He had hurt Emily deeply, left her hanging with promises he had failed to keep. He had let the thrill of the race overshadow the depth of his feelings for her. He had let her down like a Ferrari strategy. [xviii] And now, he had to face the consequences.

His reputation preceded him - the charming racer who had a different woman in every city. But Emily was not just another woman. She had seen through his façade, reached out to the person he was beneath the fame and the glory. She deserved more than just a rushed apology or a bunch of flowers. She deserved sincerity, honesty, and most importantly, a commitment that he was ready to give her.

He mulled over his options, considering everything from a grand gesture to a heartfelt letter. But none of it seemed enough. The gravity of his actions, the depth of Emily's hurt, required more than just an apology. He needed to show her that he had changed, that he was willing to put her before his career, before his fame.

As the city of the next race approached, an idea began to form in his mind. He would invite Emily to the race, not as a fan, but as his special guest. He would dedicate the race to her, show her that she was his priority, that he was willing to risk his reputation, his career, for her.

He knew it was a gamble. Emily might refuse his invitation, might not even take his call. But he had to try. Because just like on the racetrack, in love too, there was no victory without risk.

He picked up his phone, his heart pounding in his chest. As he dialed Emily's number, he realized that this was his most important race yet. And he was determined to win.

Emily was startled when her phone buzzed with an incoming call from Daniel. After weeks of waiting for this call, she was now filled with a mix of surprise, anger, and a reluctant thrill. Despite her better judgment, she answered.

Daniel's voice on the other end was different – there was a hint of nervousness, a tone of sincerity that she hadn't heard before. He apologized for his actions, for his silence, and then invited her to his upcoming race, not as a spectator, but as his special guest.

She was taken aback. A part of her wanted to decline instantly, to show him that she couldn't be swayed by a mere invitation. But another part, the part that had spent countless nights waiting for this call, urged her to give him another chance.

She remembered their night together, the warmth of his touch, the honesty in his eyes, the shared passion that was undeniable. She remembered their conversations, their laughter, their connection. And for a moment, she allowed herself to hope. But then, reality kicked in - his abrupt departure, his weeks of silence, his reputation.

She told him she needed time to think, and he agreed, his voice filled with hope. As she hung up, she was left in a whirl of thoughts. The man who had broken her heart was now trying to mend it. The man who had left her without a word was now inviting her to be a part of his world. It was a lot to process.

Part of her wanted to yell at him. To tell him that she wasn't Felipe Massa, who 15 years after crashgate was still dwelling on the past.[xix] No, she was different. She left the past in the past, and he was her past. But as much as she wanted that to be true, she was still having a hard time letting go of Daniel.

She spent the next few days in deep thought, weighing her options, analyzing her feelings. She was hurt, yes, but she also missed him. And despite everything, she knew she still cared for him.

With a deep breath, she finally made her decision. She picked up her phone and dialed Daniel's number. As she heard his voice on the other end, she gave him her answer, "I'll be there, Daniel."

Her words were met with a silence that was soon replaced by a relieved sigh. Daniel was so happy, he broke into song. "Arigato gozaimasu!" he sang at the top of his lungs, thanking her, using the few words of Japanese he had picked up over years of racing at Suzuka.

Emily was going to the race. The hurt was still there, the doubts still lingered, but for now, she was willing to give Daniel a chance, a chance to prove that he was more than his mistakes, more than his reputation. And she was willing to see where this race would take them.

The day of the race arrived, and with it, Emily. As she stepped out of the car and into the hustle and bustle of the race day crowd, Daniel was there waiting for her. The sight of him sent a jolt of familiarity through her, a reminder of why she was drawn to him in the first place.

Daniel had planned the day with meticulous care. He wanted to show Emily a side of him she had never seen, the side that wasn't always in the spotlight, the side that was just Daniel. He wanted to give her a glimpse of his world, not as a superstar racer, but as a man who had genuine feelings for her.

The day started with a private tour of the racing paddock. Emily was introduced to Daniel's team, given an insight into his pre-race rituals, and even got a chance to sit in his race car. The thrill on her face was unmistakable, and Daniel couldn't help but smile.

Then Daniel took her to the track's fake marina which was filled with fake water for a fake ride on a fake boat that he had borrowed from Guenther Steiner. With the sun warm on her skin and Daniel's neck gleaming wet from the spray of the fake water, she knew she was falling under his spell again.

Then, Daniel took her to a secluded spot near the

track, a place where they could escape the noise and the crowd. They shared a picnic under the open sky, and for the first time in weeks, they talked. Really talked. Not as a racer and a fan, but as two people who had shared an intimate connection.

Daniel was open about his feelings, his regrets, and his hopes. He didn't shy away from admitting his mistakes and promised to make up for them. He spoke of his life on the track, the highs and the lows, the victories and the losses, the fame and the loneliness. He spoke of his longing for something real, something like what he had with Emily.

As the day turned into evening, Daniel surprised Emily with a candlelight dinner in his team's hospitality suite. It was intimate, romantic, and for the first time in weeks, Emily felt a glimmer of hope. The man sitting across from her was not the playboy racer the world saw, but a man who was ready to bare his soul, to risk his heart for love.

Daniel's gestures, his honesty, and his willingness to open up were slowly chipping away at Emily's reservations. She could see the sincerity in his eyes, feel the truth in his words. And as they shared a dance under the starlit sky, Emily realized that this was not just a race for Daniel. It was his way of showing her that she mattered, that she was worth fighting for.

As the day ended, Daniel held her close,[xx] promising her a new beginning, a new race. Emily looked into his eyes, seeing a glimmer of the man she had fallen for. The path ahead was still uncertain, but for now, she was willing to take the leap, to give this race a chance. Because sometimes, even the most unexpected pit stops can lead to the most beautiful destinations.

7. THE VICTORY LAP

The roar of the crowd and the adrenaline rush of the race had faded into the background as Daniel and Emily found themselves back in the privacy of his hotel suite. Their day had been filled with laughter, deep conversations, and shared experiences, all culminating in a race where Daniel had emerged victorious. But the victory on the track paled in comparison to the victory he felt in his heart.

With the moonlight streaming in through the windows, the room was filled with a soft, gentle glow. It was in stark contrast to the harsh reality they had faced just a few weeks ago. But this time, it felt different. This time, there was a promise of something more, something real.

As Daniel took Emily into his arms, the world outside ceased to exist. It was just the two of them, lost in each other's eyes, their hearts beating in unison. He gently brushed a loose strand of hair from her face, his eyes reflecting his sincerity, his desire, his love.

Their lips met in a slow, passionate kiss, a perfect echo of their feelings. Every touch, every whisper was a testament to their deep connection, a reaffirmation of the bond that had been strained but never broken.

As they explored each other, their bodies intertwining with a familiarity that belied the short span of their relationship, they found a rhythm that was uniquely theirs. Each touch was a promise, each sigh a confession, each look a pledge. She could feel that he was harder than a Pirelli C1 tire as he crashed into her from behind like she was Max in Baku 2018.

Their night was filled with passion and tenderness, a dance as old as time yet as fresh as their feelings. They discovered new facets of each other, shared silent promises, and basked in the warmth of their shared connection.

As Daniel held Emily close, their bodies spent and their hearts full, he knew he had made the right choice. He had won the race, not just on the track, but in his heart as well. And as Emily snuggled closer, a content sigh escaping her lips, he knew he had found his home.

Their journey had been unconventional, filled with unexpected turns and pit stops. But as they drifted off to sleep, wrapped in each other's arms, they knew they were on the right track. Because sometimes, the most unexpected races can lead to the most beautiful victories. And for Daniel and Emily, this was just the beginning of their victory lap.

[xviii] Somebody please save Charles and Carlos.

[xix] GeT oVeR iT

[xx] He did not leave the space

ABOUT THE AUTHOR

Anita Driver is a Formula 1 enthusiast who has attended every Monaco Grand Prix since 1972. She first learned to love cars when her father abandoned her at a gas station at the tender age of 11. She currently resides in a cottage in New Hampshire with her 37 cats who are all named Sterling Moss. She once shared a cab with the Dalai Lama and has a very festive pink hat that she wears when she's feeling fancy.

Anita Driver graciously accepts fan mail at
authoranitadriver@gmail.com

Made in the USA
Coppell, TX
01 September 2023

21061079R00028